An Adventure for Robo-dog

Pat Thomson

Illustrated by
John Prater

OXFORD
UNIVERSITY PRESS

OXFORD
UNIVERSITY PRESS

Great Clarendon Street, Oxford OX2 6DP

Oxford University Press is a department of the University of Oxford.
It furthers the University's objective of excellence in research, scholarship,
and education by publishing worldwide in

Oxford   New York

Auckland Bangkok Buenos Aires Cape Town Chennai
Dar es Salaam Delhi Hong Kong Istanbul Karachi Kolkata
Kuala Lumpur Madrid Melbourne Mexico City Mumbai Nairobi
São Paulo Shanghai Singapore Taipei Tokyo Toronto

with an associated company in Berlin

British Library Cataloguing in Publication Data

Data available

ISBN 0 19 919477 7

1 3 5 7 9 10 8 6 4 2

Guided Reading Pack (6 of the same title): ISBN 0 19 919554 4
Mixed Pack (1 of 6 different titles): ISBN 0 19 919483 1
Class Pack (6 copies of 6 titles): ISBN 0 19 919484 X

Printed in Hong Kong

Contents

Chapter 1

Ben's Birthday

It was the night of Ben's birthday.
He was trying to get to sleep.
But he couldn't.

There was his best present, shining
and silver. It was a robot dog.
It was brilliant! It barked.
It came for its bone.
It even fell asleep
and snored.

He called it Robo-dog. Rob for short.

5

Ben got out of bed and started to play with Rob. Mum had to come upstairs three times. Then she took Rob and put him in the toy box outside Ben's room.

After that, Ben fell asleep.

At last, the house was quiet.

Everything was dark. Nothing moved.

Just after midnight, a red light glowed in the toy box.

Beep, beep, beep!

Fast asleep in his bedroom, Ben heard nothing.

Something was moving. The red light began to flash.

Chapter 2

Down the Stairs

"I'm bored," said a voice. It was a strange voice. It sounded like a computer. "Let's go, go, go."

It was the robot dog.

"Who are you?" asked a doll.

"Hi there! I'm Rob," said the dog. He wagged his metal tail.

"Well, mind my dress," said the doll. "The sparkly bits come off very easily."

"No problem," answered Rob.

"I'm Jilly," the doll added. "I belong to Sarah. That's Teddy."

A furry teddy bear in the bottom of the box sat up. He rubbed his eyes with his paws. He looked half asleep.

"So come on. Let's go and see the night life," said Rob.

Jilly and Teddy stared at him.

"What? Go downstairs?" said Jilly.
"We never go anywhere. We stay put."

"Time for a change then," said Rob,
cheerfully. "Let's go, go, go."

Jilly giggled. "All right," she said. "Let
me take off my high heeled shoes first."

Then she climbed out of the box.
She was good at climbing.

"Coming, Teddy?" Rob began to move smoothly. He was whirring gently.

"It's very dark," said Teddy.

"No problem," answered Rob. A light, set in his head, switched on. It made a bright, narrow path in front of Rob.

"That's good," said Jilly. "I want an adventure."

"Don't leave me," squeaked Teddy. He scrambled out of the box.

He did not feel very happy. He did not want an adventure. Adventures were dangerous. He sighed and hurried after them.

Chapter 3

The Cat Flap

Rob and Jilly were already downstairs.
They seemed to move easily, like Ben.
Teddy had stiff legs. Suddenly, he slipped.

Bump,

bump,

bump!

"No problem," said Rob. "Good idea
to slide. Now, how do we get out of the
house?"

"Out?" squealed Jilly. "You can't go out!" Her golden curls bobbed with excitement.

"There's a cat flap," said Teddy. "But it's not very big."

"No problem," Rob answered. "The cat flap is a good idea."

Teddy led them into the kitchen. A good idea! It made him feel quite important. He felt so important that he forgot the cat's water bowl.

SPLOSH!

"Oh, dear," said Teddy.

Rob swung his light on him. Teddy was sitting in the water bowl.

"No problem," said Rob. He helped Teddy up. "You'll dry."

Teddy plodded across the kitchen. He felt rather damp behind.

The big back door was closed, but Jilly slipped easily through the cat flap.

"Now you, pal," said Rob.

Teddy put his head through.

He could see stars. They were the sparkly bits on Jilly's dress. He put one paw through. Then the other. So far, so good. Now he could see the real stars.

Then he got stuck.

"Oh, dear," he said. "My front half is out but my back half is in."

"No problem," said Rob. His red light winked. He was thinking. Then his green light came on. "Jilly," he called, "when I count to three, pull hard."

Rob ran backwards a little. He began to whirr. All his lights flashed. "One, two, three!" He dashed at Teddy.

Rob hit the part of Teddy which was
sticking out into the kitchen. This was
nice and soft for Rob, but Rob's head was
not soft.

"Ouch!" yelled Teddy and POP!

He shot out of the cat flap. He landed on
Jilly. He could see all sorts of stars now.

As Teddy lay there, puffing, Rob came
smoothly through the cat flap.

"No problem," said Rob.

Chapter *4*

A Very Big Problem

Rob, Teddy and Jilly stood on the edge
of the lawn. It was very dark and quiet.

In the distance, an owl hooted. It was
hunting.

"So this is the Great Outdoors," said
Rob. "I've never seen it before."

"I've only seen it in daylight," said
Jilly. Her eyes sparkled like her dress.

"I don't get out much," said Teddy. "I'm an indoor type. In fact, I'm a bit scared."

"No problem," said Rob. "Bears live in woods, you know. You'll love it."

It was true, thought Teddy. He was a bear. Perhaps he'd get used to it.

Rob led the way across the grass.

Jilly gave a little cry. "Our special bush!"

Jilly showed them a gap under the bush. When they crawled in, there was a little den. There was a faded plastic tea set there.

"We used to have picnics here," sighed Jilly. "That was before Sarah and Ben went to school. I used to sit here on a rug. The toy soldiers were allowed to climb the branches."

She looked sad. "I never did."

"Climb up now," said Rob.
"No problem."

Jilly looked at him.

"Should you really?" asked Teddy.

"Yes, I should," said Jilly.

She took off her
tiara and began to climb. They
heard her grunting. The leaves rustled.

"Nearly there," she shouted.

Then, she screamed.

22

Branches crashed and shook. There
was a terrible screeching noise. Rob and
Teddy looked up.

Rob's light caught the sparkle of Jilly's
dress. Beside her, hunched on the branch,
was a big, dark shape.

Chapter 5

Night Rescue

An enormous owl sat on a branch above them. It stared down at them with huge eyes.

Teddy saw its hooked beak. Worst of all were its feet. One set of sharp talons held on to the branch. The other clutched Jilly. Her eyes were shut.

Rob whirred. He did not say, "No problem."

"Go away!" shouted Teddy.

The owl lifted its big wings and hissed. It glared at Teddy. Then it blinked and turned its head. Teddy looked at Rob's light. The owl did not seem to like the brightness.

It was then that Teddy had his best idea. He whispered to Rob. Rob nodded and started to talk. "Hi there. Good evening. I think you may have made a mistake."

The owl did not move.

"I expect you think you have a mouse there," Rob went on. "Now, I have to tell you something. Mice do not wear sparkly dresses. No, sir!"

As Rob talked, Teddy got hold of a branch. He started to climb. So that was what his claws were for! He moved very quietly. He climbed higher and higher. Soon, he was just under the owl's branch.

Poor Jilly hung down from
the owl's talons. Teddy saw her
open one eye. She let one hand
drop towards him. She gave a
tiny nod.

"Now!" shouted Teddy, and
he roared a grizzly bear roar. He
almost frightened himself.

27

Rob turned his light straight into the owl's eyes. Teddy grabbed Jilly's hand and pulled. Jilly kicked hard.

The owl raised its big wings. Then it flapped away. Jilly and Teddy tumbled down through the leaves. They sat on the ground. All three had a big hug until they felt better.

"You see?" said Rob. "No problem."

The sky looked lighter. "Time to go home," said Teddy.

"I've had an adventure at last," said Jilly. "You *were* brave, Teddy."

"Me?" said Teddy. He was amazed. They trudged slowly across the lawn.

"I shall never get through that cat flap again," sighed Teddy.

Rob pointed to an open window. "You're a great climber, Teddy. Go through that window. You'll miss out the stairs, too."

*   *   *

When Ben woke, the toys were back in the toy box. He went straight to find Rob. He did not notice Jilly, but he did notice Teddy.

"Yuk! Teddy," he said. "You're all damp." He sat him on the radiator. "Come on, Rob." He ran downstairs.

"I'm just going to have a snooze,"
said Teddy. It was lovely and warm on
the radiator. "Adventures do wear you
out, don't they?"

"They do," said Jilly. "Will you be all
right, up there?"

"No problem," said Teddy, sleepily.

About the author

Last Christmas, a friend brought a silvery, robot dog to visit. It barked, ran round the room and had a little argument with a sheepskin rug. I was sure that such a busy, bossy little dog could persuade even a comfy old teddy to go out at night and have an adventure.

My stories often start with something real which then gets turned into an adventure.

So, what do your toys get up to when you are asleep?